The Tale of Peter Rabbit

by Beatrix Potter • illustrated by Amye Rosenberg

A GOLDEN BOOK • NEW YORK

Western Publishing Company, Inc., Racine, Wisconsin 53404

Copyright © 1982 by Western Publishing Company, Inc. Illustrations copyright © 1982 by Amye Rosenberg. All rights reserved. Printed in the U.S.A. No part of this book may be reproduced or copied in any form without written permission from the publisher. GOLDEN®, GOLDEN & DESIGN®, A GOLDEN STORYTIME BOOK®, and A GOLDEN BOOK® are trademarks of Western Publishing Company, Inc. Library of Congress Catalog Card Number: 81-83346 ISBN 0-307-11950-5 ISBN 0-307-61950-8 (lib. bdg.) J nce upon a time there were four little rabbits, and their names were:

Flopsy   Mopsy   Cottontail   and Peter

They lived with their mother in a sandbank, underneath the root of a very big fir tree.

"Now, my dears," said old Mrs. Rabbit one morning, "you may go into the fields or down the lane, but don't go into Mr. McGregor's garden. Your father had an accident there; he was put into a pie by Mrs. McGregor. Now run along, and don't get into mischief. I am going out."

Then old Mrs. Rabbit took a basket and her umbrella and went through the wood to the baker's. She bought a loaf of brown bread and five currant buns.

Flopsy, Mopsy, and Cottontail, who were good little bunnies, went down the lane to gather blackberries.

But Peter, who was very naughty, ran straight away to Mr. McGregor's garden and squeezed under the gate!

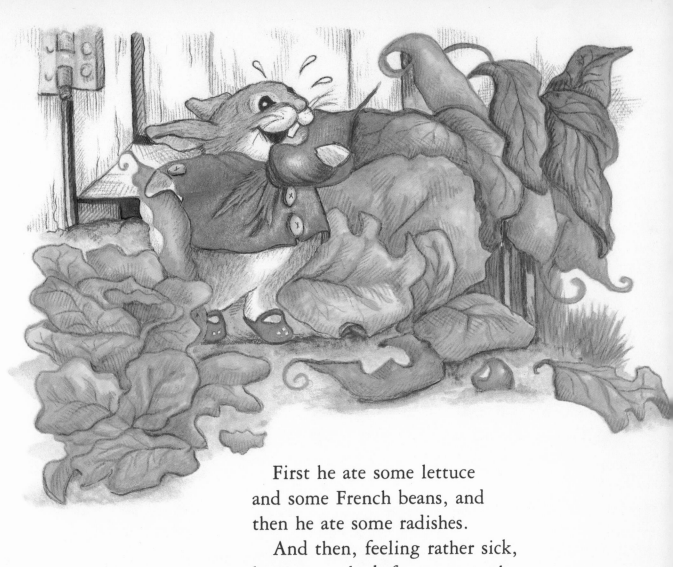

First he ate some lettuce
and some French beans, and
then he ate some radishes.
    And then, feeling rather sick,
he went to look for some parsley.

But round the end of a cucumber frame, whom should he meet but Mr. McGregor!

Mr. McGregor was on his hands and knees planting out young cabbages, but he jumped up and ran after Peter, waving a rake and calling out, "Stop, thief!"

Peter was most dreadfully frightened. He rushed all over the garden, for he had forgotten the way back to the gate. He lost one of his shoes among the cabbages, and the other shoe amongst the potatoes.

After losing them, he ran on four legs and went faster, so that I think he might have got away altogether if he had not unfortunately run into a gooseberry net and got caught by the large buttons on his jacket. It was a blue jacket with brass buttons, quite new.

Peter gave himself up for lost and shed big tears. But his sobs were overheard by some friendly sparrows, who flew to him in great excitement and implored him to exert himself.

Mr. McGregor came up with a sieve which he intended
to pop upon the top of Peter. But Peter wriggled out just
in time, leaving his jacket behind him...

and rushed into the toolshed
and jumped into a can.

It would have been a beautiful
thing to hide in, if it had not
had so much water in it.

Mr. McGregor was quite sure that Peter was somewhere
in the toolshed, perhaps hidden underneath a flowerpot.
He began to turn them over carefully, looking under each.
Presently Peter sneezed—*Kertyschoo!*

Mr. McGregor was after him in no time and tried to put his foot upon Peter, who jumped out of a window, upsetting three plants. The window was too small for Mr. McGregor, and he was tired of running after Peter. He went back to his work.

Peter sat down to rest. He was out of breath and trembling with fright, and he had not the least idea which way to go.

After a time he began to wander about—going lippity, lippity, not very fast, and looking around.

He found a door in a wall, but it was locked, and there was no room for a fat little rabbit to squeeze underneath.

An old mouse was running in and out over the stone doorstep, carrying peas and beans to her family in the wood. Peter asked her the way to the gate, but she had such a large pea in her mouth that she could not answer. She only shook her head at him. Peter began to cry.

Then he tried to find his way straight across the garden, but he became more and more puzzled. Presently, he came to a pond where Mr. McGregor filled his watering cans. A white cat was staring at some goldfish; she sat very, very still. But now and then the tip of her tail twitched as if it were alive. Peter thought it best to go away without speaking to her; he had heard about cats from his cousin, little Benjamin Bunny.

He went back towards the toolshed, but suddenly,
quite close to him, he heard the noise of a hoe—
scr-r-ritch, scratch, scratch, scritch.

Peter scuttered underneath the bushes. But presently,
as nothing happened, he came out and climbed upon a
wheelbarrow and peeped over. The first thing he saw was
Mr. McGregor hoeing onions. His back was turned towards
Peter, and beyond him was the gate!

Peter got down very quietly off the wheelbarrow and started running as fast as he could go along a straight walk behind some black-currant bushes. Mr. McGregor caught sight of him at the corner....

But Peter did not care. He slipped underneath the gate and was safe at last in the wood outside the garden.

Mr. McGregor hung up the little jacket and the shoes for a scarecrow to frighten the blackbirds.

Peter never stopped running or looked behind him till
he got home to the big fir tree. He was so tired that he
flopped down upon the nice soft sand on the floor of the
rabbit hole and shut his eyes. His mother was busy
cooking; she wondered what he had done with his clothes.
It was the second little jacket and pair of shoes that Peter
had lost in a fortnight!

I am sorry to say that Peter was not very well during
the evening. His mother put him to bed and made some
camomile tea, and she gave a dose of it to Peter!
"One tablespoonful to be taken at bedtime."
But Flopsy, Mopsy, and Cottontail had bread and milk
and blackberries for supper.